Topps LEAGUE Story

STEAL THAT BASE!

· **BOOK TWO** ·

By **Kurtis Scaletta**

Illustrated by **Eric Wight**

Amulet Books
New York

For Byron, who stole our hearts.

Special thanks to Sean, T.J., and
Dylan of the Saint Paul Saints.
—K.S.

To Ethan & Abbie.
—E.W.

Cataloging-in-Publication data has been applied for and
may be obtained from the Library of Congress.

ISBN: 978-1-4197-0287-7 (hardcover)
ISBN: 978-1-4197-0262-4 (paperback)

Book design by Chad W. Beckerman

Printed and bound in U.S.A.
10 9 8 7 6 5 4 3 2 1

Amulet Books are available at special discounts when
purchased in quantity for premiums and promotions as
well as fundraising or educational use. Special editions
can also be created to specification. For details, contact
specialsales@abramsbooks.com or the address below.

ABRAMS
THE ART OF BOOKS SINCE 1949
115 West 18th Street
New York, NY 10011
www.abramsbooks.com

CHECKLIST

☐ **#1 JINXED!**

☐ **#2 STEAL THAT BASE!**

☐ **#3 ZIP IT!**

☐ **#4 THE 823RD HIT**

It was five minutes before midnight and the bottom of the ninth inning, and I was about to break a promise.

I was a batboy for the Pine City Porcupines. When I took the job, I promised my parents I would try to be home by ten o'clock and would *never* work past midnight. "That's just too late for a boy your age," Dad had said.

But there had been a rain delay and the game started late. The Porcupines were tied with the Attica Finches, 3–3. If the Porcupines didn't score here, the game would go into extra innings.

I'd also made a life-long promise to my uncle Rick that I would never leave a baseball game before it was over. Uncle Rick took me to a game when I was six. The Porcupines fell behind by ten runs, and I wanted to go home. "If you leave early, you might miss a thrilling comeback," he'd told me. "You might miss a walk-off home run. Never leave before the last out, Chad."

"I won't," I told him, and I meant it. The Porcupines ended up losing that game, but they did get a grand slam in the eighth inning. We would have missed it if we hadn't stuck around.

Tonight there was no way to keep both promises unless the Pines scored really soon.

Victor Snapp's deep voice boomed over the speakers. "Now batting: the designated hitter, Sssssammy Ssssssolarisss!" Victor Snapp had been the announcer for the Pine City Porcupines since before I was born. He was my idol. I wanted to be a baseball announcer when I grew up.

"Come on, Sammy!" I shouted. Sammy was the best hitter on the team.

He swung at the first pitch. The ball sailed into the outfield. The Finches' center fielder ran after it.

"It's a gapper!" said Victor Snapp. He said that whenever a ball got between two outfielders. My heart nearly leaped out of my chest.

The ball hit the fence and rolled back toward the outfielder. Sammy took a big turn at first base, then stopped.

I went to fetch the bat.

"Solaris stretched that double into a single!" I heard someone shout. It had to be Ernie Hecker. Ernie had the biggest mouth in Pine City, and he always shouted stuff at the players and umpires. This time he was right. Most baseball players would have reached second base easily on a hit like that.

Sammy took his lead off first. The pitcher didn't even look at him. There was no way Sammy would try to steal a base.

"Now batting: the first baseman, Teddddddddy Larrrrrabeeeee!" Victor Snapp announced.

Teddy hit the ball hard, and it sailed to the right field corner. The outfielder caught it. Sammy took a couple of steps toward second, then changed his mind and stayed at first.

The crowd groaned again. Most runners would have tagged up and advanced a base.

"Now batting: the right fielder, Danny O'Brien!" Victor announced.

Sammy must have heard the crowd boo, because he did something crazy. The pitcher threw an off-speed pitch to Danny, and Sammy took off. He kicked up a cloud of dust and started toward second.

Danny didn't swing. The catcher threw the ball to second. The second baseman took two steps off the base to catch it. He ran back to the base and tagged Sammy.

Sammy was out by a mile.

"I could have stolen that base from up here!" Ernie Hecker shouted.

"Sammy Solaris is caught stealing!" said Victor Snapp. "And so we head to the tenth inning."

Sammy returned to the dugout and slumped onto the bench.

"Good try, Sammy," I told him.

"Nice of you to say that," he said.

"I didn't signal for you to steal a base," said the Pines' manager. His name was Harry Humboldt, but everybody called him Grumps.

"You'll know when I do, because it'll be never. That's when it'll happen. *Never.*"

"Ah, come on. I just thought I'd get into scoring position," Sammy replied.

I missed the rest of their talk because Wally tugged on my sleeve. "You got a phone call."

Wally was the clubhouse manager. He was my boss.

"Thanks. It's probably my dad. I'll have to go home."

"That's all right," Wally said. "You should go home. We want you kids fresh for tomorrow."

I went back to the locker room to take the call. The phone was the old-fashioned kind, with the receiver wired to the base and the base stuck to the wall.

"I'm waiting out in front," said Dad. "Are you ready?"

"I just have to change."

"Hey, ask Dylan if he wants a ride too," said Dad.

"Sure."

Dylan was the other batboy for the Porcupines. He was working in the Finches' dugout for tonight's game. We took turns helping the opposing team.

"See you in a sec," I told Dad.

I changed clothes, grabbed my baseball card binder, and went to the Finches' dugout.

Even though he's a batboy, Dylan isn't a big baseball fan. I showed him my baseball card collection sometimes—well, *part* of it: I had more than 5,000 cards! I told him about my favorite players. I explained plays during the game. Dylan didn't know it, but he was my secret mission: By the end of the season, I was going to make him the greatest fan of the world's greatest game!

8

I found Dylan sitting on the edge of the bench in the visitors' dugout.

"Hey." I nudged his elbow.

"Shh." Dylan pointed at something.

I scanned the infield and didn't see anything unusual.

"What?"

"It's right there!" He pointed again, and I realized he was pointing at the fence that protected the dugout from foul balls. I set my baseball card binder down and knelt by the fence to get a better look.

There was a little creepy-crawly thing sitting on the chain link.

"It's just a bug," I said.

"It's not a bug. It's a spider," said Dylan.

"Spiders are bugs."

"Not exactly. They're arachnids. Bugs are insects. Hey, look. It's spinning a web."

"Great," I said. "Wally said we should go home. My dad will give you a ride."

"Thanks," Dylan replied. "I want to stay and watch. I can call my parents later."

"I thought baseball bored you."

Dylan had admitted that when we first started working for the Porcupines.

"I mean watch *that*," he said. He nodded at the spider.

"Of course."

I knew Dylan liked animals, but did a spider count as an animal?

Just after I got home I had one of the worst moments of my whole life. I'd forgotten my card binder! I'd left it in the Finches' dugout when I was talking with Dylan about that stupid spider. It felt like I'd left my right arm somewhere.

I called the Finches' locker room. Dylan answered.

"It's me. Is the game still going on?"

"Yeah. And Sparky is done with his web!"

"Sparky?"

"Sparky the Spider."

"You named that thing?"

"No, I just call him Sparky."

"That's naming him!"

"Maybe. By the way, you left your binder here."

"I know—that's why I called. I wanted to make sure it was OK."

"It's fine. Do you want me to put it in your locker?"

"Keep it overnight," I said. "Take good care of it. But feel free to look through it. There're some cool cards in there."

"Sure," Dylan promised. "Gotta go. I want to see if Sparky's caught any bugs yet."

• • •

I overslept the next morning. We batboys had to be at the ballpark two hours before the game started. I would have to hurry to get there on time.

It was my own fault. I'd listened to the rest of

the game on the radio before I went to sleep. The Porcupines finally won in the thirteenth inning. Tommy Harris hit a triple, and Mike Stammer brought him in with a sacrifice fly. It would have been so great to be there. I knew what Uncle Rick meant about never leaving a game early. Too bad Mom and Dad didn't understand.

I got dressed, bounded down the stairs, and ate a bowl of cereal.

Mom saw me put the bowl in the dishwasher.

"Do you need lunch?" she asked.

"I can get a hot dog at the ballpark."

"You've been eating a lot of hot dogs lately," she said. "Why don't I pack you a lunch while you walk the dog?"

"Oh, yeah." It was my job to walk our dog in the morning. Penny was near her food bowl. She looked up at me with great big eyes and made a whimpering noise.

"Hi, girl." I reached for the food bin.

"She's already had breakfast," said Mom.

"Aw, Mom. She wants more," I said. Penny was still staring at me. "It would make her happy."

"She's happy when she's eating a second breakfast," said Mom. "She's not happy when she's all out of breath on a short walk."

"She just has little legs." I took a handful of kibble and put it in my pocket.

Mom didn't notice. "Walk the dog while I make your lunch," she said.

I could still be on time if I hurried. I put the leash on Penny and took her out for a quick trot around the block.

Mom was right—Penny was panting before we got to the corner. She was getting kind of roly-poly these days. She was still cute, though.

"Hi, Chad!"

I turned and saw Abby. She waved at me

from across the street. Abby worked for the Pines too, and was in my grade at school. She ran across the street to meet us.

"I'm going to the ballpark early," she explained. She reached out and let Penny lick her hand. "It's a big day. They're giving out bobbleheads. Hey, aren't you supposed to be there by now?"

"I'm leaving as soon as I'm done walking the dog." I took the dog food from my pocket and fed it to Penny.

"I'll walk to the ballpark with you," said Abby.

"We're going to have to walk fast," I told her. Usually I rode my bike.

"No problem. I can walk superfast."

We took Penny home, and Mom gave me my lunch. I peeked at it. It was pasta salad and baby carrots.

"There's not even a cookie," I said.

"Just eat your lunch first," said Mom. "If you're still hungry, you can see if they have something at the ballpark that's halfway good for you."

"All right."

"Have fun and work hard," Mom said. She planted a smooch on top of my head. I was glad Abby had waited outside.

• • •

Abby and I walked six blocks, crossed a field, waited for one traffic light, crossed the street, and turned the corner.

We stopped.

"Holy cow!" said Abby.

There were about a billion people crowded around Pine City Park.

"There are always lines on bobblehead day," I told her.

"But the game doesn't even start for two hours!"

"They're *Spike* bobbleheads," I reminded her. Spike was the Porcupines' new junior mascot. He was the biggest star of the season. Everybody loved that quill-covered porcupine kid. "Not everyone will get one," I added. "They're 'only available while supplies last.'"

"They must really want those bobbleheads," said Abby. We both knew something most people didn't: Abby was Spike. She put on a porcupine costume and played the part. She was great at it.

We started across the parking lot.

"Dad!" a little girl tugged on her father's shirttail. "Those kids are cutting!"

"Hey, what's the big idea?" the man asked.

"We're with the Pines," I said. "I'm a batboy."

"And I work in fan services," said Abby.

"Oh, I see," the man said. "Sorry for bothering you." He let us go past.

"No fair!" said the little girl.

"It's all right, Petunia," her dad said. "They work for the team."

"But it's not fair!" she said again. "They'll get the last two Spike bobbleheads. I just know it."

"No, they won't, Petunia," her father said.

"Show me your ticket, so I can see your seat number," Abby said to the girl. "I'll make sure you get a Spike bobblehead."

"Promise?" Petunia asked.

"Promise," said Abby.

"You can believe it," I added. "Abby and Spike are good friends."

3

I t's you!" said Wally when I got to the locker room. Several of the players were getting suited up for the game.

"Yeah. Sorry I'm late," I said. I put my lunch in the team fridge. "Mom wanted to make me lunch, I had to take the dog for a walk, and the line outside was really long."

"I'm just glad you're here," said Wally. "I wasn't sure either of you boys would make it after that marathon last night."

"You mean Dylan isn't here yet?"

Dylan had never been late before.

"His mother called and said he wasn't feeling well. Maybe he's just tired. I know I am."

Maybe he got bit by that spider, I thought. Maybe he wasn't "sick." Maybe I'd be working with Spider-*Boy* . . . That could be cool! Still, I hoped Dylan didn't feel too bad.

"I'll hold down the fort here," said Wally. "You go help the Finches. I know you'd rather help the Pines, but we're in a jam."

"No problem."

"And here, take this. I was only able to get one," said Wally. "You're here, so it's yours. At least now there won't be a fight over it." Wally pulled a white box out of the traveling case and handed it to me.

"All right!" I guessed what it was right away. I slid out a Spike bobblehead and unrolled it from the Bubble Wrap. I gave the

little porcupine head a tap and set it nodding. Awesome!

"Hey! Hey, Chad," said Sammy Solaris. "Don't forget about my corn dogs before you go, buddy."

I rewrapped the bobblehead and stowed it in my locker. "No problem," I said. I fetched Sammy two corn dogs before every game.

"Do you ever think about having something besides corn dogs?" asked Teddy Larrabee, the first baseman. "Like a regular hot dog, or a chili dog, or a Chicago-style hot dog, or a Carolina-style dog, or a bratwurst . . ."

"Or a frankfurter?" said Wayne Zane, the catcher.

"A frankfurter *is* a hot dog," said Teddy.

"I'm just sayin'," Wayne replied.

"I like corn dogs," said Sammy. "That's my thing. I eat two corn dogs before every game."

"You don't want to mess with tradition," said Wayne. "Especially when you're hitting like Sammy."

"Listen to him," said Sammy. "He's wise."

"By 'wise,' he means 'old,'" said Wayne.

"I agree about traditions," said Lance Pantaño. "Every time I pitch, I drink four cups of coffee before the game. And only from this." He took a big gulp from a Porcupines mug. The mug had an old piece of tape on it that said "Property of Lance."

"If I drank that much coffee, there'd be a seventh inning stretch in every inning, and I'd be spending it in the bathroom," said Mike Stammer.

"That's why I drink only four cups when I pitch," said Lance. "When I'm not pitching, I'm a nine-mug man. Nine innings, nine coffees."

"What about last night's extra innings?"

asked Wayne. "Wouldn't thirteen coffees keep you up all night?"

"Decaf," Lance replied.

"I don't know how you can have *anything* before a game," said Tommy Harris, the third baseman. He was the newest and youngest Porcupine player. He'd just come up from rookie league. "I'm too nervous to eat."

"I'm too hungry to be nervous," said Sammy. He looked at me and patted his stomach.

"On it, Sammy," I said. "I'll go get your corn dogs."

I ran out of the locker room and out to the plaza. The gates were now open, and the fans were swarming in. A lot of people were carrying Spike bobbleheads. Kids shook the toys and made the porcupine's oversized head rock back and forth.

The woman at the food stand saw me and

waved me up to the counter. I didn't have to wait in line. That was one of the perks of working for the team.

"Corn dogs, coming right up!" she said even before I ordered. She knew that Sammy Solaris had corn dogs before every game.

The smell of hot food made my stomach rumble, but I'd promised Mom I'd eat healthier today.

I forgot to tell the woman at the counter that. She set down three corn dogs and winked. Two were for Sammy, but the extra corn dog was always for me.

I hurried back to the Pines' locker room and gave Sammy all three dogs.

"You get an extra today," I said. "My mom made me lunch."

"But that's not the tradition," said Sammy. "I eat two corn dogs before every game. Not one corn dog. Not three corn dogs. *Two* corn dogs." He held up two fingers.

"Well, just imagine what you can do if you eat three," said Teddy.

"Don't mess with tradition," said Wayne.

"Traditions have to start somewhere," said Teddy. "Maybe you'll hit for the cycle. Maybe you'll steal a base."

Sammy's eyes got wide. "You think so?" He dipped one of the dogs in mustard and took a bite.

"You never know until you try," said Teddy.

"I tried stealing yesterday," said Sammy. "It didn't go so hot."

"But you only had two corn dogs."

"Don't mess with Sammy's system," said Wayne. "He eats two corn dogs, and he gets a lot of doubles and homers. It works for him."

"I do need to steal a base, though," said Sammy.

"You don't *need* to," said Wayne.

"Yes, I do," said Sammy. "On the last off day, I visited my niece's softball team. I was giving them a pep talk, and I told them they could do anything if they set their mind to it. Later on my niece asked me, 'Uncle Sammy, did you ever steal a base?' I said no. She asked me why not, and I said I wasn't that kind of player. So she said, 'If you put your mind to it, you can do it, right?' What could I say? I said, 'Yeah, of course I can.'

"So she said, 'Do it this weekend, Uncle Sammy,' and I said I would. That's why I tried it last night."

"Sweet story," said Wayne. "But a corn dog isn't going to help you run faster, unless you're chasing a corn dog truck."

"You're hilarious," said Sammy.

"Just sayin'," said Wayne.

"You've never stolen a base?" Tommy asked in surprise. "I've only been with the team a month, and I've stolen five!"

"Yeah, yeah. I know," said Sammy. "You're a jackrabbit out there. I just need to steal one base this weekend so I don't let down Wendy. That's my niece."

"Tell her you hit a lot of homers," said Myung Young. "Those are better than stolen bases."

"He's right," said Danny O'Brien. Or maybe it was Brian Daniels. I always got those two guys confused. Their names were similar, and they looked the same: unruly red hair and big freckled noses. "Tell Wendy you just set your mind to hitting home runs," said Danny or Brian.

"It's not just Wendy," said Sammy. "I want to prove to *myself* that I can steal a base."

"So take one from the equipment room," said Wayne.

Sammy glared at the catcher.

Zane shrugged. "I'm just sayin' . . ."

"You're no help," said Sammy. "But I know who will be. I'll get Chad the batboy to help me."

I popped my head up. "Who, me?" What was I supposed to do?

"Yeah. You gave a magic baseball card to Mike Stammer. That card helped him turn an unassisted triple play."

"Sure did," said Mike. "I haven't had a single error charged against me since I got it." He patted his hip pocket to show he still had the card I'd given him.

"The baseball card isn't *magic*," I said. "It's just a reminder that . . ."

"Listen, batboy." Wayne leaned in and

whispered in my ear. "If Mike thinks it's a magic card, then it's a magic card."

"I don't need a card as powerful as Mike's," said Sammy. "It just has to be a little bit magic. Stealing a base is a lot easier than turning a triple play all by yourself."

"It doesn't hurt to try," said Mike. "Who else do you have in that binder?"

"Rickey Henderson," said Brian or Danny. "That's who you want. Henderson stole more bases than anyone else in the history of baseball."

"Or Ty Cobb," said Myung Young. "He was famous for stealing bases."

"I don't have a Ty Cobb card," I said. "Ty Cobb played a hundred years ago. His cards are worth a fortune."

"How about Ichiro Suzuki?" asked Tommy. "Or maybe Juan Pierre? Those guys steal a lot of bases and they're still playing. It can't be that hard to find their cards."

"Good choices," said Myung.

"I do have an Ichiro card, but I don't have it with me," I said.

"Hey, look," said Sammy. "I'll take Kenny Lofton or Carlos Beltran. Anyone who ever stole a base."

"I don't have *any* baseball cards with me," I said. "I can go to the gift store and buy a pack. Maybe you'll get lucky and get one of those guys."

"Nah, I think the card has to be from that red binder of yours," said Sammy. "That's what makes it magic."

I started to say, "They're not magic," but then I remembered what Wayne had whispered to me.

"Let me settle this!" Grumps's voice rattled

the lockers. The Porcupines' manager stomped over to the group. He wagged a finger in Sammy's face. "If I don't give you the sign, you better not try to steal a base."

"But you never give me the sign," said Sammy.

"Exactly," said Grumps. "You're a slugger That's your role." Grumps patted Sammy's shoulder. "Just go out there and slug, all right?"

"Oh, all right," said Sammy. He didn't look happy about it.

I grabbed my lunch and set off for the other dugout.

"Good luck, Sammy," I whispered on my way out.

The Attica Finches were warming up, so I had to walk the long way around the diamond.

"Chad . . . Chad . . . Hey, Chad!"

I turned. There was a porcupine right behind me. Spike came close enough to whisper. "Remember the little girl outside?" Abby said. "I promised her a bobblehead?"

"Yeah. Her name is Petunia."

"Petunia!" Abby snapped her fingers. "I couldn't remember her name."

"How can you forget a name like Petunia?"

"I just remembered it was a flower. I was thinking Rose, Lily, or Violet."

"Those are normal names," I said. "I've never heard of anyone named Petunia that wasn't a cartoon character. And a pig."

"I think it's a pretty name," said Abby. "But I don't have a bobblehead to give her."

"*You* didn't get one? But you're Spike!"

"I know! But the bobbleheads are all gone. Every last one."

"Well, maybe Petunia got into the ballpark before they ran out."

"No way," Abby said. "She and her dad were way at the back of the line, remember?"

"Oh, yeah." I thought about the bobblehead back in my locker. I really wanted to keep it. I wanted to collect things from my time with the Porcupines. I already had a signed baseball that Mike Stammer gave me.

"I shouldn't have said I'd get her a bobblehead," said Abby. "She'll say Spike broke a promise. It'll be in the newspaper. 'Junior Mascot Lies to Little Girl.'"

"It won't be in the newspaper," I said.

"Well, what if she goes home sad? What if she never wants to come to another game?" Abby's voice rose higher. "What if she ends up hating the Porcupines?"

"You're right. This is serious . . . Hmm. I have a bobblehead you can give Petunia. I mean, if you can't find one any other way. I have to go work the Finches' dugout, but I can get it during the seventh inning stretch."

"Promise?" Abby asked.

I gulped. "Sure."

"Thanks, Chad! You're

a hero!" Abby remembered she was in costume, and shouldn't shout. "Thanks," she whispered.

• • •

There was a note taped to the fence in front of the Finches' dugout.

Please don't do anything to this spiderweb. The spider worked really hard on it.

Thanks, Dylan

P. S. It is not the kind of spider that bites people.

The web was still there, and so was the spider. I saw it hiding under one of the links in the fence. Dylan would be happy.

The Finches finished practicing and came back into the dugout.

One of the players sat down and pulled the brim of his cap over his eyes. "Last night's game went way too late."

"Tell me about it," said another player.

"Yawn."

"Zzzz."

Two seconds later, everybody had to jump up for "The Star-Spangled Banner," and then it was time to play ball.

Lance Pantaño was pitching for the Pines. He struck out the first batter.

"Nice breeze blowing back here!" Ernie Hecker hollered from the stands.

The next batter for the Finches took an awkward swing at the first pitch and bounced the ball to the shortstop. Mike Stammer fielded the ball and threw to first for the out. He'd been great on defense lately. There were rumors that he would get called back up to the big leagues any day now.

Lance got ready to throw his next pitch, but nobody was in the batter's box.

"Wake up Jonny!" a Finch shouted.

"Yo, Jonny!" A player reached out and tugged on his teammate's foot. "You're batting."

"What? Oh." Jonny got up, pushed his cap back, rubbed his eyes, and headed for the plate.

"You'll need this." I handed him his bat.

"Oh, yeah. Thanks."

"Hey, pitcher!" Ernie Heckler hollered. "Take it easy on this guy. He looks like he just woke up."

Jonny yawned and tapped his bat on the plate. The pitch sailed past him. Jonny didn't even lift his bat off his shoulder.

"Umpire, make sure that guy is still alive!" shouted Ernie.

Jonny stepped back and watched another pitch zoom by.

"Strike two!" the umpire shouted. Jonny had forgotten to ask for a timeout. He swung at the third pitch but missed it by a mile. He headed for the dugout and started to sit down.

"That's three outs, Jonny," said the Finches' manager. "Time to play defense."

"Oh, right." Jonny put on his catcher's gear and headed toward the plate.

"Stay awake out there," shouted the manager. "Don't let them catch you napping."

Usually that's just a saying, but with this guy it could happen! It might be a good day to steal a base—even for Sammy Solaris.

I ate my lunch while the Porcupines batted. The pasta salad was OK, but it was no corn dog. The baby carrots would have been better with nacho cheese.

Sammy batted fourth in the inning. Tommy Harris was on third and there were two outs. The pitcher walked Sammy on four pitches. It was baseball strategy. If Sammy got a hit, Tommy would score. But since the bases were not loaded, Tommy couldn't score on a walk.

Now would be a good time to steal second. If

the catcher's throw to second base wasn't perfect, the runner on third could come home. They call that a double steal. I looked over at Grumps standing in the Porcupines' dugout. Sometimes he'd slap his legs and his shoulders and tug on the brim of his hat. It was a sign to the base runner. It might mean "steal a base" or "run on contact."

There was no sign this time. Grumps just stood there and stared at Sammy Solaris. I knew that look from Mom and Dad. It meant: Don't even think about it.

Sammy didn't budge.

Wayne Zane flied out on the first pitch. Then Mike Stammer struck out, and the inning was over. Sammy Solaris didn't get one foot closer to stealing a base.

Victor Snapp's deep voice bellowed over the speaker system. "Please welcome the Porcupines' senior and junior mascots . . . Pokey and Spike!"

The crowd cheered. The two porcupines rolled out in a golf cart and stopped in the infield.

Spike jumped out of the cart and set down a giant boom box. The little porcupine pushed a button and rap music blared. Spike danced and the crowd clapped.

Pokey covered his ears and shook his head. He climbed out of the cart and punched a button on the boom box. The music died.

The crowd played along. They booed Pokey.

Pokey covered his ears but finally gave in and turned the music back on. Spike started dancing again. Everyone cheered.

"I'm with the big porcupine," Ernie Hecker shouted. "This song is terrible!"

Spike looked up to where Ernie was sitting and thumbed his porcupine nose. The crowd loved it.

5

ustavo Perez, the Finches' first baseman, poked at the dugout fence. The spider dropped to the turf and scurried away.

"What are you doing?" I asked.

"Trying to smoosh that spider," Gustavo said. "Did you see where it went?"

"No—don't!"

"Look, kid, spiders get smooshed sometimes. And I don't like spiders."

"I know, but Dylan likes that spider."

"Who's Dylan?"

"He's the other batboy. He's the one who

wrote that note." I pointed at the paper taped to the fence.

"'It is not the kind of spider that bites people,'" Gustavus read aloud. "How does your friend know?"

"Because he's really good at science," I said.

"Spiders eat insects," the Finches' pitcher said from the bench. His name was Todd Farnsworth. "I'll bet this one gobbles up gnats and mites. Would you rather have gnats and mites in your face, Gus?"

"No," Gustavo admitted.

"Then leave the kid's pet spider alone."

The Finches' catcher was sitting next to him. He yawned and rubbed his eyes. "Maybe that thing can play in the outfield," he said.

We all looked at him.

"It can catch flies. Get it?"

"Go back to sleep, Jonny," said the pitcher.

Not much happened for the next two innings. In the bottom of the fourth inning, a couple of the Finches' bench players asked me to fetch some sunflower seeds.

"Three bags of sunflower seeds," I told the woman at the food stand.

"That's all the Finches want?"

"Yep."

"They're named for birds and they eat like birds," she said. "Anything for you?"

"Sure." I remembered what Mom had told me. "I need something halfway good for me."

"We have tropical fruit kebabs."

"Tropical fruit ke-whats?"

"Tropical fruit kebabs. They're new." She took a skewer from the cooler and handed it to me. It had pineapple chunks and bananas and jumbo marshmallows and some orange-colored fruit that wasn't oranges.

"What's that?" I pointed at one of the orangey chunks.

"Mango."

I nibbled at a piece of mango. "It's good."

"Take some kebabs back to the players," she said. "Nobody's ordering them, and the fruit won't keep." She loaded a cardboard tray with fruit kebabs.

I took it all back to the dugout and set the tray down on the bench. I nibbled on my own tropical fruit kebab and watched the game.

There was nobody out, and Sammy was on first base after a clean single to left field. He took a step off the base and looked at the Porcupines' dugout for the sign. Grumps gave him his stone-faced look again. Sammy stepped back on the bag.

It was for the best, because Wayne got a hit and Sammy got to second anyway.

Later in the inning either Danny O'Brien or Brian Daniels hit a double.

"He's faster than a skyscraper!" shouted Ernie Hecker as Sammy lumbered home. It was a run for the Porcupines! The crowd cheered.

When the inning ended, I crossed the field to pick up a bat. Sammy stopped me. "Hey, Chad, never mind about that magic baseball card. I can't use it. Coach won't let me steal a base."

"Maybe he would if the situation was right?"

"No way. He won't ever give me the sign. I'll just have to tell my niece that you can do anything if you put your mind to it *and* Grumps lets you do it."

"I'll find you a card anyway," I promised.

"Thanks, Chad." Sammy headed back to the Porcupines' dugout.

Either Brian Daniels or Danny O'Brien

grounded into a double play, and the Finches came back to the dugout to bat. It was the top of the fifth inning.

Todd Farnsworth, the Finches' pitcher, picked up one of the fruit kebabs.

"Where did these come from?"

"The kid brought them," a player said. "Try one. They're good."

"I never liked marshmallows, but I could go for some fruit," said Todd. He slid off a marshmallow and started to toss it toward the trash.

"Hey, what are you doing?" said Gustavo. "That's the best part." He took the marshmallow and popped it in his mouth, then grabbed a skewer and took off more marshmallows. He popped them all into his mouth at once.

Todd ate a couple of pieces of fruit off the skewer. "These are great! You guys should try them." He pushed the tray down the bench.

Several of the players took one.

Gustavo mumbled something.

"We can't hear you, Gus," said the shortstop. "Your mouth is full of marshmallows."

Gustavo pointed at the shortstop's fruit kebab, then at himself.

"Gus wants all of your marshmallows," Todd explained. The players started handing him their marshmallows. Gustavo couldn't keep up.

"Perez, you're supposed to be on deck!" the manager shouted. Gus stuffed the marshmallows into his pocket and headed out of the dugout.

"Hope he doesn't have to slide," said Todd. "Could get messy."

Gustavo hit a home run to tie the game.

"Pass me a marshmallow," said the second baseman.

ylan showed up during the seventh inning stretch. The game was still tied, 1–1. The fans were singing "Take Me Out to the Ball Game," with Ernie Hecker's voice rising above the rest of the crowd.

"I thought you were sick," I told Dylan. I was putting some bats away. "Is getting well quick one of your new spider powers?"

"Nah, Mom just wanted me to get more sleep," he said. "After I got up, I decided to web-sling my way over here. How's Sparky?"

"Er . . . OK, I guess." I put the last bat

away and went back to the Finches' dugout.
Dylan was right behind me.

"You can go back to the Pines' dugout if you
want," he said. "I'll help the Finches."

"Sure," I said.

Then I realized that Dylan had frozen in
place, his mouth wide open.

"He's gone!" Dylan pointed at the empty
web. "Sparky is gone!"

"He might come back."

"Nobody smooshed him, did they?"

"Nobody smooshed him," I said. "That
spider just dropped and ran away. I saw him
do it."

"I hope he's all
right," said Dylan. He
crouched and peered
through the fence at the
infield.

"I gotta go," I said. I had to hurry to the Porcupines' dugout, because the Pines were going to bat. "I'll let you know if I see Sparky."

I watched for spiders on my way around the diamond, but didn't see any. I did bump right into Spike.

"Hey!" said Abby.

"Sorry."

"Never mind. So, um . . . I can't find another bobblehead for Petunia." Abby said. "Can I still have yours? You did promise."

"I know." When I'd made that promise, I was sure Spike could find a Spike bobblehead. No such luck. "Let's go get it."

Abby followed me into the Porcupines' dugout.

"Hey, Spike is here!" Wayne Zane gave Spike a high five.

"You're great, Spike," said Tommy. "You crack me up every time."

Spike toed the ground and looked bashful.

"Be right back." I ran and fetched the porcupine bobblehead from my locker. I opened the box to make sure the toy was still in there. That bobblehead would have looked great on my bookshelf, right next to my baseball cards. I was sad to lose it.

"Make sure Petunia takes good care of this," I said when I handed the box to Spike.

The mascot did a huge exaggerated bow, then gave me a Porcupine hug, which is like a bear hug, only you've got to watch the quills. Spike didn't leave the dugout, though.

"What's wrong?"

The little porcupine tugged on my arm and pulled me off to the side where nobody could hear us.

"I forgot Petunia's seat number," Abby whispered.

"Oh, no!"

"Do you remember it?"

"No, I didn't even look at the tickets." I bit my lower lip and thought about it. "Maybe you can go into the stands and find her. It's not that big a ballpark."

"There isn't much time left in the seventh inning stretch," Abby replied. "What if I don't find her?"

"I have an idea. Can you be batboy for a few seconds?"

"I don't know how."

"Just make sure that the bat for the next batter is ready, and return the bat to the rack when he's done. The players' names are on the bats, and you can match up their names to the numbers on the lineup card . . . "

"Whoa, slow down," said Abby.

"No time. Do the best you can," I said. I ran through the locker room and out onto the concourse. I had to talk to my idol.

• • •

Victor Snapp sat in a booth in between the upper and lower decks, directly behind home plate. The door was propped open. He was hunched over a scorecard, making flecks with his pencil for every pitch. "Remember," he said into the microphone, "Teddy 'the Bear' Larrabee is today's Papa's Pizza Pick to Click. If Larrabee gets a hit in today's game, fans will receive a five-dollar coupon good on any large pizza."

Victor's voice was deep and booming and smooth all at the same time. I practiced talking like that all the time but never came close.

I'd only met him once, when I crashed into him and spilled nacho cheese all over his shoes. What if he remembered me? What if he was still mad?

I'd have to try. He could make an announcement: "Petunia, please pick up your bobblehead from Spike at the Fan Services booth after the game." I didn't know her last name, but how many Petunias could there be at one ball game?

Teddy knocked a fastball over the head of the third baseman.

"There it is!" said Victor. "A base hit for the Bear! The Porcupines have a base runner, and you have a five-dollar coupon good for any large pizza at Papa's Pizza. And it looks like Spike the Porcupine is fetching the bat! Now I've seen everything."

He saw me by the door, hit a button on the microphone stand, and waved me in.

"You're that batboy," he said.

I gulped. He did remember me. "I am. I'm sorry I spilled food on you. It was my fault."

"It takes two to bump into each other," Victor said. He offered me a handshake. His hand was huge, and it buried my hand whole. "Pleased to finally meet you," he said.

"Me too!" I said. "I'm a big fan. I want to be a baseball announcer when I grow up."

"You don't say? Do you want to announce the next batter?" he asked.

"What?"

"Just say his name. It's written down right there." He pointed at his scorecard.

"I know who's batting!" I said. "I set up the bat rack enough times."

"So go for it," Victor said. He pushed the microphone at me and undid the mute button.

I remembered all the times I practiced at home. I could do this. I made my voice deep and booming. "Now batting for the Porcupines: the left fielder, BRRRRIAN DANNNIELS!" I heard my own voice echoing over the speakers. It was amazing.

Victor grabbed the microphone. "Of course he means the *right* fielder, *Danny O'Brien*!" He hit the mute button.

"Ulp. Sorry," I whispered. I always got those two confused.

"Easy mistake," Victor told me. "Anyone could make it." He picked up his pencil.

"Thanks," I said. I hung my head and went back down to the Porcupines' dugout. I was so mad at myself, I forgot to ask Victor to make the announcement.

7

I hoped that nobody noticed my mess-up. That hope didn't last long.

"I heard your voice on the speakers," Abby whispered as soon as I got back to the dugout.

"Huh? It must have been some other kid."

"It sure sounded like you. What did you do? Did you find Petunia?"

"No, I kind of blew it," I admitted. "But we still have two more innings."

"I'll go greet fans and try to spot her," said Abby. She tucked the box with the bobblehead under her arm. "I'm off to find Petunia."

"Good luck."

"Never say that to an actor. It's bad luck. You're supposed to say 'Break a leg.'"

"How about 'Break a quill'?"

"Perfect!"

Spike went out onto the field and waved at fans, then went up the stairs to shake hands with people.

I watched the game. The Porcupines were still batting. It sure was a long inning, but the Porcupines hadn't scored. Everything was just taking forever. I saw Gustavo reach into his pocket, then pop something in his mouth. He was still eating marshmallows, even while he was playing!

Sammy Solaris sat down next to me.

"Hey, was that you on the PA system?"

"Nope," I lied. "It was some other kid."

"Nah, it was you," said Sammy.

"OK, yeah. It was me. I messed up the name. I got Brian confused with Danny."

"Ah, don't worry about it," said Wayne. "Even they can't tell each other apart—can you, Danny?" He looked at a player returning to the dugout.

"I'm Brian."

"See what I mean?" said Wayne.

The seventh inning was finally over. Most of the players grabbed their gloves and headed back to the field. Sammy stayed behind because he was the DH, or designated hitter. The DH hits instead of the pitcher.

"Now pitching for the Porcupines . . . Nate Link!" said Victor Snapp.

Nate is what they call a sidewinder. Instead of pitching overhand, he pitches from the side.

He threw a few warm-up pitches to Wayne Zane behind the plate. Wayne had to reach way out to catch one. He didn't look too happy.

"Uh-oh. Looks like Nate doesn't have his best stuff today," said Sammy.

Pokey and Spike came out and played catch with an oversize baseball. Spike kept throwing the ball far away from Pokey. When Pokey ran to get the ball, Spike turned to the audience and grinned. The fans laughed.

"I can give you a baseball card now," I told Sammy. "Dylan brought me my binder."

"It doesn't matter," he said. "I'll have to tell Wendy that her uncle can't steal a base no matter how hard he puts his mind to it. Even if I get to bat again, and even if I reach base, Grumps will never give me the sign."

"He might," I said. "In the right situation."

I got the binder and flipped through the

pages. I looked at the stat for SB, or stolen bases.

"If you do give me one, it doesn't have to be a world-class base stealer," said Sammy. "Just someone who steals a base once in a while."

"How about this guy?" I gave him my 2010 Bengie Molina card.

"Ha. Good one," Sammy said, but he handed the card back to me.

"What's wrong?"

"Molina's a good hitter and a great catcher. But he's a slow runner. If me and him and a snail and a turtle were in a race . . ." Sammy thought it over. "Well, the turtle would win, but I'd beat the snail and Bengie Molina."

"That's the point! He's still stolen a few bases." I showed Sammy the back of the card. "See? Three stolen bases. And this doesn't show the one he stole in the playoffs."

"He must have gotten lucky."

"Maybe. Or maybe the situation was just right. Anyone can steal a base in the right situation."

"I don't know." Sammy looked at the card. "You know, I do like Bengie. He's a great player. I like all three of the Molinas." Bengie had two brothers who also played Major League Baseball. All three Molinas were catchers. "So if Bengie can steal a base, I can too?" he asked.

"In the right situation," I told him.

"How do I know when that is?"

"You'll get the sign."

"The sign from the manager?" Sammy asked.

"Yeah."

"I heard that," said Grumps from the other end of the bench. "Don't hold your breath."

"Just wait for the right situation," I whispered.

"All right," Sammy whispered back. "Me

and Bengie are going to steal a base for Wendy."
He tucked the card in his pocket.

Grumps didn't say anything, so I guess he
didn't hear *that*.

• • •

The first batter for the Finches in the top of
the eighth inning was Gustavo. He popped a
marshmallow in his mouth, went to the plate,
and hit his second home run of the game.

"Now we're losing," said Sammy. "I don't
like that."

"Him and his marshmallows," I said.

"What?"

"Nothing. It's just a fluke." I didn't want to
give Sammy any ideas. He couldn't steal a base
if he filled up on marshmallows.

Spike came back to the dugout before the
next batter got to the plate.

"Your porcupine friend is here again," said Sammy.

"Yeah." I stood up so Abby could whisper to me.

"I can't find Petunia anywhere," she said. "It's just a sea of people. And she's so small. What am I going to do?"

Did I dare go back to Victor Snapp? I gulped. Did I have a choice? Hmm . . . I did.

There was one other person at the ballpark practically everyone could hear.

"I'll be right back," I told Abby.

I went to the seating area above the visitors' dugout. I was looking for the man with the loudest mouth in all of Pine City: Ernie Hecker.

I knew his voice, but I didn't know what he looked like. I had never met him. I only knew his name because everybody knew it. "There goes Ernie Hecker again," people would say every time he hollered.

I needed something to happen. Something Ernie would *have* to comment on.

Sammy was right. The Pines' pitcher, Nate

Link, did not have his best stuff going on. He'd given up that home run to Gustavo, and then he had walked a batter. Nate was one pitch away from walking the next batter.

He threw ball four. The batter took first, and the runner on first moved to second.

I waited for Ernie to yell something snarky. He didn't. Everyone in the section was just watching the game.

Maybe Ernie had left early?

The next batter stepped into the box. It was Jonny, the sleepy catcher. Nate sped a fastball by him. The umpire called it a ball. The next pitch got by the catcher (*both* catchers) and rolled to the backstop. Wayne went to get it.

"That's a wild pitch," said Victor Snapp, "and Wayne Zane seems to have tripped over somebody crawling around in foul territory."

I leaned over the dugout fence and craned

my neck to see what was going on. Dylan was crawling around in the dirt between the dugout and the backstop. The umpire tapped him on the shoulder. Dylan stood up, and the umpire spoke to him.

"It's a batboy," said Victor Snapp. "A batboy was crawling around in foul territory. What was he doing?"

"HELPING NATE LINK FIND THE PLATE!" Ernie Hecker answered.

Every single person in the ballpark must have heard him. A lot of them laughed.

And I had found my man. Ernie was in the third row. He wore glasses and a red polo shirt and was mostly bald.

"Excuse me." I edged past some fans and got to Ernie. The seat next to him was open.

"Hi," I said. "Can I please sit here a minute?"

"Help yourself," said Ernie. "It's my brother's seat, but he's not here today."

I sat down. Dylan was walking back to the visitors' dugout with his shoulders slumped.

"So, who are *you*?" asked Ernie.

"I'm your second biggest fan," I told him.

"I'm an accountant. Accountants do not have fans."

"I'm a fan of the stuff you say during the game. You know, like that joke you just made."

"It's called *ballpark patter*," he said. "I do take pride in my patter. I admit it."

"Your ballpark patter is great," I said.

The woman on the other side of me looked at me and shook her head.

"Anyway, I'm your second biggest fan," I told Ernie. "Your *first* biggest fan is my friend Petunia. Will you please wave to her? It would make her day."

"Who's Petunia?" Ernie asked.

"She's right over there." I started to point

and stopped. "I don't know where she is," I said. "But if you just say 'Hi, Petunia!' She'll hear you."

"'Hi, Petunia'?"

"Yeah."

"You want me to say 'Hi, Petunia.' What's the joke?"

I shook my head. "No joke."

"There must be," said Ernie. "It's like when I ask you for a henway."

"What's a henway?"

"Three or four pounds." He laughed and slapped his knee.

I thought about it. "No, it's not like that."

"Or like when I say, can you lend me a hammerfor."

"What's a hammerfor?"

"Pounding!" He laughed even harder at that one.

"It really isn't a joke," I told him. "Please say 'Hi, Petunia.' She'll hear you and wave, and then you wave back."

"No way am I doing it," Ernie said. "I am not saying 'Hi, Petunia.'"

"Please?"

"Hi, Petunia. Hi, Petunia. Hi, Petunia." He repeated it several more times. He was loud even when he wasn't trying. "Is that supposed to sound like something else? I don't get it."

"Look." The woman next to me pointed. A little girl was standing on the steps, three sections over. She was looking our way. She waved.

I waved back.

The little girl waved again.

I saw a big *G* on the stair. I counted: ten rows back.

Petunia!

Ernie didn't wave.

"She's my biggest fan?" said Ernie. "She's only four years old, tops."

"Yeah. Thanks!" I said. I rushed through the row—"Excuse me, excuse me"—and back to the aisle.

"I still don't get it!" Ernie shouted after me.

9

By the time I got back to the Porcupine's dugout, the score was 4–1, *not* in the Pines' favor. And the Finches were still batting.

Abby was fielding a foul ball, which wasn't easy to do in a porcupine costume. The fans laughed and clapped for her.

"Section G, ten rows back," I told her.

"Great," she said. She grabbed the box with the bobblehead, bolted from the dugout, and ran across the field. She forgot the inning was still going.

The second base umpire tried to stop her, but she ran right past him. The fans cheered.

"Spike is storming the field," said Victor Snapp. "The game is in a brief delay while an umpire chases a porcupine across the field. And now I really have seen everything."

Spike reached the seating area steps and ran up. The second base umpire went back to his spot on the field.

The mascot bounded up the steps and gave Petunia the bobblehead. The little girl jumped up and down and then gave Spike a big hug.

Nate Link pitched, and the batter bounced into a double play. The inning was finally over.

"The Finches get three runs on four hits," said Victor Snapp. "The inning also had two walks, a wild pitch, a distracted batboy, and a disruptive mascot. Figure out how to put that on your scorecards! We go to the bottom of the eighth inning."

It was mostly a happy ending, except for the fact that the Porcupines were losing—and I didn't have a bobblehead.

• • •

George "President" Lincoln batted first for the Porcupines. He was the second baseman. He hit a single. Tommy was next, and he hit a single, too. Myung came to the plate and grounded out. The runners were able to advance, so at least the Porcupines had two runners in scoring position.

Mike Stammer hit a double, and the crowd went wild as both runners scored. Now the Porcupines only needed one more run to tie the game, and there was a runner at second base.

Sammy Solaris came to the plate. The crowd stood up and clapped.

He took a ball, then swung at the next pitch and missed, then hit a foul ball.

I felt my stomach tie up in knots. Sammy had been on base every at-bat this game. What were the odds he could do it again?

He swung and smacked the ball. It soared toward the fence. The crowd gasped.

The ball hit the fence and bounced back. That was enough to score Mike Stammer. Sammy turned at first base.

"Go! Go! Go!" people shouted at Sammy, but he didn't go.

The center fielder fielded the ball and threw to the second baseman. He had an arm like a cannon. Maybe Sammy made the right choice by staying put. If he'd tried to go to second, he might have been out.

Grumps turned back to look at the bench. He nodded at Luis Quezada, a utility infielder and pinch runner. Luis leaped up. Grumps was taking Sammy out of the game. He went to signal to the umpires that he was putting in a replacement. He stopped and brushed at his leg. He slapped his left thigh three times. He drummed his fingers on his right shoulder. He took off his cap and swiped at his shoe while hopping on one foot.

I didn't know the signs, but Sammy's eyes lit up.

Todd was still pitching. He glanced at Sammy, saw he was still on base, and turned back to face Wayne Zane at the plate. He pitched.

Sammy took off.

The crowd roared. Grumps turned purple.

Wayne didn't swing. The catcher fumbled with the ball.

Sammy kept on running. He was halfway to second base.

Jonny finally got a grip on the ball and flung it to second. The second baseman caught it and braced himself to tag Sammy.

Sammy put on the brakes and started back to first.

Grumps covered his eyes.

Gustavo, the Finches' first baseman, caught the ball and got ready to tag Sammy as he bolted back to first. Sammy stopped, turned, and headed back to second.

"They have Sammy picked off," said Victor Snapp.

It was the slowest rundown I ever saw. Sammy strode to second. The second baseman toed the bag and waited for Gustavo to throw back the ball.

Gustavo took a few steps, and pumped. But he didn't throw the ball. He took another few steps and made like he was going to throw, but

the ball didn't leave his hand. He gave up and started running after Sammy.

Sammy slid. The second baseman got out of the way. Sammy's heel reached the bag a split second before Gustavo caught up and tagged him. The second base umpire signaled . . .

SAFE!

"He's safe!" Victor Snapp shouted. "Sammy Solaris just stole second base! That's the first stolen base in his career. What a game!"

The crowd stomped and cheered.

The Finches' pitcher shook his head in disbelief. Gustavo tried to throw him the ball, but still couldn't get it out of his hand.

Todd had to go take it by force. He glared at the ball and tossed it to the umpire for another.

Gustavo wiped his hand on his pants, and suddenly I knew what had happened. He couldn't make the throw because he had a hand full of marshmallow goo!

Grumps called a time-out and sent Luis to pinch-run for Sammy. Sammy got a standing ovation as he came in from the field. He was beaming. His smile could have lit up a night game.

"I stole second base," he said.

"I can't wait to call Wendy!"

"I didn't give you the sign to steal," Grumps barked.

"It sure looked like you did. You touched your leg and took off your cap. That's the sign, coach. All that other stuff was funny to watch, but it didn't change the sign."

"I had a spider on me! I was shaking it off," Grumps said. "Can't you tell the difference?"

"I can't see a spider all the way from first base," said Sammy.

"Bah."

"Coach, it's OK," said Sammy. "I was safe. All's well that ends well."

"You got lucky."

"I'll take lucky," said Sammy. "Or magic." He patted his hip pocket and gave me a thumbs-up sign, then went to the locker room to call his niece.

I started to ask Grumps what happened to the spider, but decided it was not a good idea. He was called Grumps for a reason.

Wayne Zane hit a long single, and Luis Quezada sped home. The Porcupines took a one-run lead. Ryan Kimball, the Porcupines' closer, started warming up in the bull pen. Teddy Larrabee struck out, and then either

Danny O'Brien or Brian Daniels flied out to right field.

"The Porcupines get four runs on five hits, and the strangest stolen base I've ever seen," said Victor Snapp. "So we go to the top of the ninth!"

I went to the dugout door and searched the ground. I didn't see Sparky. I didn't see a dead spider, either, so that was good news.

10

Dylan and I searched the field for an hour after the game. We found plenty of bugs but no spiders.

"You know," I said, "a spider is pretty small, and a ballpark is really big."

"I know," Dylan replied. "What's one little spider, anyway? There are billions of spiders in the world."

But he kept searching the grass.

"I'm going home," I said. "I have to get back in time for supper." I stood up and jogged toward the locker room. Just in the nick of time, I spotted a tiny black splotch against the white line around the on-deck circle. I almost smooshed it but stopped short. I hopped a couple of times before I got my balance. I knelt and took a closer look. Something wiggled. It could have been Dylan's spider, but it was hard to be sure.

"*Psst.* Dylan." I waved him over and pointed.

"Is that Sparky?"

"I think so." He put his hand out and let the spider crawl into his palm.

"And you're sure it's not the biting kind?"

"Yep. Unless you're an insect," said Dylan. "I'm going to move him outside the ballpark. Too many people stamping around in here."

"That's all baseball is to you?" I asked. "People stamping around?"

"I guess it is fun sometimes," Dylan admitted. The spider tried to crawl out of his hand. He swapped it into his other hand. "When the two guys were chasing Sammy back and forth. And when the mascot tore across the field. That was awesome."

"Yeah. Those sure were highlights. And you know, when Sparky makes a web. That's pretty awesome, too."

"Well, it's not exactly a high-speed chase," he said.

"Neither was that rundown!"

He laughed. "Thanks for helping me find Sparky," he said. "I just like animals. No matter how small. Some people don't get it."

"It's not much different being a big fan of Single-A baseball," I told him.

• • •

There was a green car parked in our driveway. I saw it from the corner and took off running. I would know that car anywhere, even before I saw the ballpark bumper stickers plastered all over it.

"Uncle Rick!" I shouted, banging through the front door.

"Hey, it's the all-star batboy!" Uncle Rick jumped up to give me a hug. He looks like Dad, but with more hair and less stomach. It turned out he'd just arrived, and Mom and Dad hadn't even known he was coming. Uncle Rick lives in the city. He explained that he'd been driving back from a trade show and took a detour to surprise us.

Uncle Rick is the biggest baseball fan I

know. He's the one who explained the rules of the game to me when I was little, and taught me all the ballpark slang, and showed me how to keep score. He even gave me all his baseball cards. That was huge. I knew Uncle Rick loved those cards. "They just sit around at my place," he'd said. "I don't have much time to enjoy them, but you do."

When Uncle Rick goes on vacation, he figures out a route where he can see as many baseball games in as many different ballparks as he can. Some years he goes to spring training in Florida or Arizona. I hope one day he'll take me with him. Uncle Rick has a great life for a grown-up, even if he spends most of his days selling dental supplies.

Over dinner I told Uncle Rick all about being a batboy. I told him about Grumps's nickname and Wally's mustache and Wayne

Zane's bad jokes. I told him about Mike Stammer's unassisted triple play and Sammy Solaris's stolen base.

"You never know what's going to happen," Uncle Rick said. "That's why I never leave until the game is over."

"I did leave a game before it was over," I admitted. "It was just last night. I missed a great walk-off hit."

"I made him do it," Dad explained. "It was way past his bedtime."

"Well, do what your parents say, even when they're wrong." Uncle Rick winked and got himself some more spaghetti. "I left a game early once," he admitted. "I found out later the pitcher finished a no-hitter. I could have been there for a historic moment, but I left after only four innings."

"*Why?*" I couldn't believe that Uncle Rick

of all people would leave in the middle of a no-hitter.

"I found out my nephew was coming, and I wanted to be there to meet him," he said.

"What?" I was his only nephew, and I didn't remember that. Then I realized what he meant—the day I was born.

"I can't believe you missed a no-hitter for *that*," I told him.

"Well, it was only the fourth inning," he said. "I didn't *know* it was going to be a no-hitter . . ."

Mom and Dad laughed, but I think Uncle Rick was being serious.

11

ncle Rick spent the night. We have a small house, but the couch in the office pulls out into a bed.

"Are you driving home after breakfast?" I asked him.

"Well, I was hoping to see a ball game," he said. "I want to root for my favorite batboy. I just hope there is a game." He pointed out the window at dark, gloomy clouds. "It looks like a big storm is coming."

Sure enough, it started drizzling when I was out walking Penny. I tried to jog home, but she started panting and I had to slow down.

"Sorry, girl. I forget how short your legs are." She used to keep up with me, but my legs used to be shorter. Besides that, she was getting plump. Mom was right.

We were both damp when we got home.

"Did Wally call?" I asked. I was afraid they'd canceled the game already.

"Nope," said Dad. He was in his favorite chair, reading a thick book about farming in the Middle Ages. He's always reading thick books about weird things.

"Are you coming with us?" Uncle Rick asked him.

Dad shook his head. "Sorry. I'll be at the next game. I really want to finish this book. There's another one I want to get to."

"Is it about the history of the rutabaga?" Uncle Rick guessed. "Or how worms worm?"

"Fungi," said Dad. "It looks really interesting."

"Well, at least a book has never been called on account of rain," said Uncle Rick. "Let's go, Chad!"

• • •

The ticket office wasn't open yet, but the guard let both of us in.

"Morning, Chad!" he told me. I felt pretty cool leading a grown-up past the gate and into the "Employees Only" entrance.

"I've never been behind the scenes like this," Uncle Rick said.

"Really?"

"I've been to a lot of ballparks, but I've never seen the guts of one," he admitted.

"Wow." I couldn't believe it. I could actually teach Uncle Rick something about baseball!

Wally had just made coffee, and the

machine was whistling and blowing steam.

"Wally, this is my uncle Rick. Is it OK if I give him a tour?"

"It's all right with me, as long as you get everything done," Wally said. "There probably won't be a game, anyway. They just never call it until the last minute."

Some of the players were sitting on the benches in the locker room.

"Hey, guys, this is my uncle Rick."

"Teddy Larrabee." Teddy shook his hand. "You got a good batboy for a nephew."

"He's not only good, he's great," Mike Stammer said. "I'm Mike Stammer."

"You're the one with the unassisted triple play!" Uncle Rick said.

"Yep," said Mike.

"Chad's more than great," said Wayne. "He's outstanding in the field. Especially during batting practice. Ha! Get it?" Nobody laughed. "Just sayin'," he added.

"And you must be Wayne Zane," said Uncle Rick.

• • •

There was a bolt of lightning and a crash of thunder during batting practice. It started to pour. We ran off the field so the crew could roll out the tarp. Uncle Rick had gone to buy his ticket, but he'd probably have to take a rain check.

Sammy was in the dugout studying the Bengie Molina card.

"Can I keep this a while longer?" he asked.

"I guess." I didn't like breaking up my page of Molina brothers in the binder. "If you think it'll help you steal another base."

"I don't need to steal another base," said Sammy. "I just wanted to steal one in my career, and now I have. But I see here that Bengie's got five triples." He pointed at the stats on the card. "I think he hit another one since then, too. I want to hit a triple before I'm done."

"Did your niece put you up to it?"

"No, I wanna do this one for me." Sammy tucked the card into his pocket. "By the way, I think I'll skip the corn dogs today. I need to put my mind to dropping a few pounds."

I started setting up the bat rack, knowing it was probably for nothing.

"The game is now postponed," Vincent Snapp announced over the PA system. "You can exchange your ticket stub for any remaining Porcupines' game this season. Thanks for coming, and try to stay dry!"

I hoped that Uncle Rick had made it to the ticket office. If he had bought a ticket, then he'd have to come back this summer and see a game.

Dylan came running from the other dugout.

"Guess we get a day off," he said. "But I hope Sparky's all right out there."

"Spiders can take a little rain," I said. "If they couldn't, there wouldn't be any spiders left."

• • •

Abby caught me and Dylan on our way out of the ballpark. She was dressed like Abby, not like Spike.

"Oh, good. You're still here." She flipped the hood of her rain poncho. We stood under the overhang by the gate, where it was dry. I could see Uncle Rick's green car in the distance. He flashed his lights to show he'd seen us, and started cruising across the lot to get us.

"This is for you." Abby handed me something damp. It was covered in plain white paper with baseballs drawn on it.

"Wow. Thanks. What is it?"

"Yeah, what's that?" Dylan asked.

"Chad gave me his Spike bobblehead so I could give it to a little girl. She loved it, by the way! I wanted to make it up to you . . ."

I tore open the paper. There was a white box. The same box the bobblehead had come in!

"You found another one?" I asked Abby. I opened the box. There was something inside, bundled in Bubble Wrap. I unrolled it. "Where did you get another bobblehead? Oh!"

I was holding a misshapen, handmade Spike bobblehead made of modeling clay. It was the kind of clay you dry out in the oven.

Abby hadn't found another bobblehead. She'd *made* one.

"I did the head separate, so it bobbles," said Abby. "See?" She gave it a tap. "My dad helped me put the pieces together."

The head wiggled—not really a nod, more like the clay porcupine was trying to shake water out of its ear.

"It's awesome!" I said.

I had something rarer and cooler than a Spike bobblehead. I had the only Spike bobblehead in the world that was made by Spike!

About the Author

Kurtis Scaletta's previous books include *Mudville*, which *Booklist* called "a gift from the baseball gods" and named one of their 2009 Top 10 Sports Books for Youth. Kurtis lives in Minneapolis with his wife and son and some cats. He roots for the Minnesota Twins and the Saint Paul Saints. Find out more about him at www.kurtisscaletta.com.

About the Artist

Eric Wight was an animator for Disney, Warner Bros., and Cartoon Network before creating the critically acclaimed *Frankie Pickle* graphic novel series. He lives in Doylestown, Pennsylvania, and is a diehard fan of the Philadelphia Phillies and the Lehigh Valley Iron Pigs. You can check out all the fun he is having at www.ericwight.com.

Come On into the **Topps®** Reading Clubhouse!